Kaley,

Enjoy your
dining experience &
Love & God bless,

Auntie Sheeba
&
Uncle Jim
October 1996

The
Search for the
Atocha Treasure

The Search for the Atocha Treasure

Fran O'Byrne-Pelham
and Bernadette Balcer

Dillon Press
New York

Collier Macmillan Canada
Toronto

Maxwell Macmillan International Publishing Group
New York   Oxford   Singapore   Sydney

Library of Congress Cataloging-in-Publication Data

O'Byrne-Pelham, Fran.
The search for the Atocha treasure.

Bibliography
Includes index.
Summary: Discusses the sinking of the Spanish galleon Nuestra
Señora de Atocha off Key West, the discovery of the treasure-
laden wreck in 1985 by treasure hunter Mel Fisher, and the archeological importance of the finds.
1. Nuestra Señora de Atocha (Ship)—Juvenile literature. 2. Trea-
sure-trove—Florida—Juvenile literature. [1. Nuestra Señora de
Atocha (Ship) 2. Buried treasure. 3. Underwater explora-
tion] I. Balcer, Bernadette. II. Title.
G530.N83028 1989
975.9'41   88-20201
                                                                  CIP
                                                                  AC

ISBN 0-87518-399-9

Macmillan Publishing Company, 866 Third Avenue
New York, NY 10022

Printed in the United States of America
  2 3 4 5 6 7 8 9 10

To our families

Acknowledgments

As we wrote this book, we found there were many times when we needed the help and reassurance of friends and family. We found, too, that we made new friends as we explored libraries and told others of our project.

Our special thanks go to R. Duncan Mathewson, who in spite of a hectic schedule, found time to send us materials and photographs and to lend support. Joe Bereswill receives our thanks for his terrific photographs, too. Likewise, the photographers of the Mel Fisher Maritime Heritage Society, Inc.—Don Kincaid, Pat Clyne, and Scott Nierling—have our deepest appreciation for lending us their excellent photographs.

To Bill Trantham, Corey Malcom, and the secretaries in Florida, we also say thank you. The academic world was warm and interested.

Mr. Thomas Schneider, our editor, became a valued and trusted advisor, and we thank him sincerely.

The librarians in the Philadelphia Free Library and Abington Library were very helpful, as were our friends at Delaware Technical and Community College.

To Mary, Michael, and Don Pelham and to Patrick, Sarah, and Pat Balcer—thanks for listening and reading and making us laugh.

Contents

Facts

Historical Facts about the *Atocha*

The Ship

Built in 1620 in Havana, Cuba, under the direction of
Alonso Ferreira, shipmaker.
Weighed 550 tons; supported 20 bronze cannons.
Kind of vessel: A three-masted galleon, or warship.

Important Dates

September 4, 1622	The *Nuestra Señora de Atocha*, in a fleet of 28 ships, sets sail for Spain from Havana, Cuba.
September 6, 1622	A hurricane pushes the fleet toward the Florida Keys. The *Atocha*, smashed against the coral reefs, sinks, carrying 260 people to their deaths.
September 12, 1622	The Marquis de Cadereita hires Gaspar de Vargas to salvage the wrecks of the *Atocha* and the *Santa Margarita*, both sunk in the hurricane. After several months, de Vargas gives up the search for the *Atocha*.
June 1626	The king of Spain gives Francisco Núñez Melián a contract to salvage the ships. Melián has a 680-pound (309-kilogram) diving bell cast for the search. Melián finds the *Margarita*, but not the *Atocha*. His search documents are sent to Seville, Spain, where they are placed in the archives.

1817	The United States buys Florida from Spain. All records of Spanish shipwrecks are moved to Seville.
1969	Mel Fisher, owner of a dive shop and part-time treasure hunter, begins searching for the 1622 fleet. Eugene Lyon, a researcher, helps Fisher find vital clues in old Spanish documents.
June 12, 1971	Mel Fisher finds an ancient anchor off the Marquesas Keys near Florida. No identification can be made.
July 1973	Mel Fisher's son, Kane, finds a silver bar whose numbers match those of a bar loaded onto the *Atocha*.
July 10, 1975	Dirk Fisher finds nine bronze cannons from the *Atocha*.
June 1980	Mel Fisher finds the treasure and the ruins of the *Santa Margarita*, sister ship of the *Atocha*.
July 20, 1985	Mel Fisher's crew discovers the remains of the *Atocha*.
October 1986	Forty of the *Atocha*'s timbers are transported to a lagoon at Key West Community College.

Introduction

In 1622 a ship heavily laden with gold and silver for the king of Spain left the harbor in Havana, Cuba. Caught in a hurricane near Florida, the *Nuestra Señora de Atocha* sank; most of the passengers lost their lives. For more than 350 years, the vessel lay on the sea bottom within forty miles of Key West, Florida, until it was discovered by a treasure hunter named Mel Fisher.

The finding of the *Atocha* meant at least $200 million worth of treasure for Fisher, his team of divers, and his investors to share. Mel Fisher's company, Treasure Salvors, salvaged 115 gold bars, 78 gold chains, 32 tons of silver, more than 3,000 emeralds, thousands of silver coins, and many precious artifacts—tools, ornaments, and other objects from an earlier time—from the wreck. Yet, just as important as the treasure in gold, silver, and emeralds was the discovery of another treasure—the hull of a seventeenth-century ship.

Archeologists, the scientists who study artifacts to learn about past human life and activities, were thrilled. Finding the *Atocha* meant that they could reconstruct the ways that seventeenth-century shipbuilders built their galleons. In addition, the ship would provide information on how the Spaniards dressed, ate, and lived on a ship that sailed three centuries ago.

This book tells the story of the galleon *Nuestra Se-*
ñora de Atocha's sinking. It also tells how marine science,
inventions, engineering wonders, and even library research contributed to the finding of that ship.

We have based our book on the story of the *Atocha*
as it is recorded in several sources. In retelling the story
of the ship's sinking, we often had to imagine the words
that the characters spoke to one another, since this information was not available. Likewise, when we wrote
about the divers and the scientists who worked to find
the *Atocha*, we sometimes had to reconstruct their
words.

The story of the sinking and the finding of the *Ato-*
cha is true. It is also an incredible adventure that links
twentieth-century treasure hunters and scientists with a
time centuries ago when Spanish ships carried the wealth
of the New World to support a royal empire.

-1-

A Treasure
Fit for a King

In the eerie stillness of the deep, blue water, a scuba diver glided easily over a huge spray of elkhorn coral. A long, silver barracuda eyed him curiously, and then moved on. The diver surveyed the underwater world through his mask, while exploring the ocean bottom with a metal detector.

As he approached a cluster of seaweed waving in the current, the needle on the meter bounced wildly. Sending the sand swirling, he dug a hole in the ocean floor. In the filtered rays of sunlight, he saw the unmistakable glint of gold. Unable to yell because of his mouthpiece, but feeling the thrill of his discovery, he reached to touch the gold. It was a link, joined to a seven-foot (two-meter) chain that had rested in the seabed for more than three hundred and fifty years.

Close by, another diver, excited by the steady pulse-beat of his metal detector, reached his gloved hand into

A diver uncovers a gold chain on the sea bottom—part of the treasure in gold and silver that sank with the *Atocha*.

the sand. In a sweeping motion, he uncovered hundreds of old Spanish coins—pieces of eight. He scooped them by the handful into his mesh bag, stopping for a moment to check the pressure gauge on his air tank. A ten-minute supply of air remained. He looked toward his diving partner and raised his hand to signal that it was time to surface. Together, scattering the sea animals that had come to graze on the algae loosened by the divers' digging, they swam toward the anchor line.

Jerry E. Hammond, Sr.

Silver pieces of eight, six, and four.

Breathing steadily, the two divers rose slowly through the fifty-five feet (seventeen meters) of seawater. As they surfaced, they tore off their masks and mouthpieces, and shouted to the crew of the waiting treasure salvor, *Dauntless*.

The first diver to the ladder offered the gold chain to an excited crew member. The other diver strained to lift the bag with the silver bulging through its netting. On board, the crew photographer grabbed his camera and, focusing carefully, took the first pictures ever made of the treasure. Others unstrapped the scuba tanks and helped the two divers out of their wetsuits. They all talked at once: "Is there more?" "What's there?" "Did you see the ship?" "Is it the *Atocha*?"

"Radio Mel," someone shouted. The captain picked up the microphone of his ship-to-shore radio and announced, "Mel, this is the *Dauntless*." "Come in," Mel radioed back. Quickly, the captain relayed to Mel Fisher, director of this salvage expedition, the news of the newly discovered treasure.

The crew recorded the site on special graphs. Then, they pulled up anchor and steered the *Dauntless* to their home port in Key West, Florida. For the divers, the undersea discoveries of Memorial Day 1985 were a sign that a huge treasure was within reach—a treasure Mel Fisher had been searching for for almost twenty years.

The Treasure Map

Among those interested in the discoveries of the *Dauntless* crew was Eugene Lyon. Lyon, a researcher, had been working on a history project in a library in Spain in 1970 when he uncovered something exciting. Among the worm-eaten documents he was examining was a salvage report from the year 1626. The crumbling paper told how a man named Francisco Melián had attempted to recover the riches of a ship called the *Nuestra Señora de Atocha* ("Our Lady of Atocha"). The Spanish galleon had sunk near the Florida Keys in a hurricane in 1622. Lyon knew that his friend, Mel Fisher, had been searching for that wreck for four years. After many hours in the library unrolling brittle parchments, Lyon discovered clues that would help his friend find the treasure he was searching for.

As Lyon translated the ancient script, he read about a time more than three centuries ago when Spanish ships carried the wealth of the New World across the Atlantic Ocean to Spain. The king needed the gold and silver to pay for a war Spain was fighting in Europe. During the trip across the Atlantic, the ships faced dangers from raging hurricanes and from pirates in search of treasure. In September 1622, an armed fleet prepared to leave from Cuba for the long journey to Spain.

This is the story of that fateful journey.

Mel Fisher on the ship-to-shore radio.

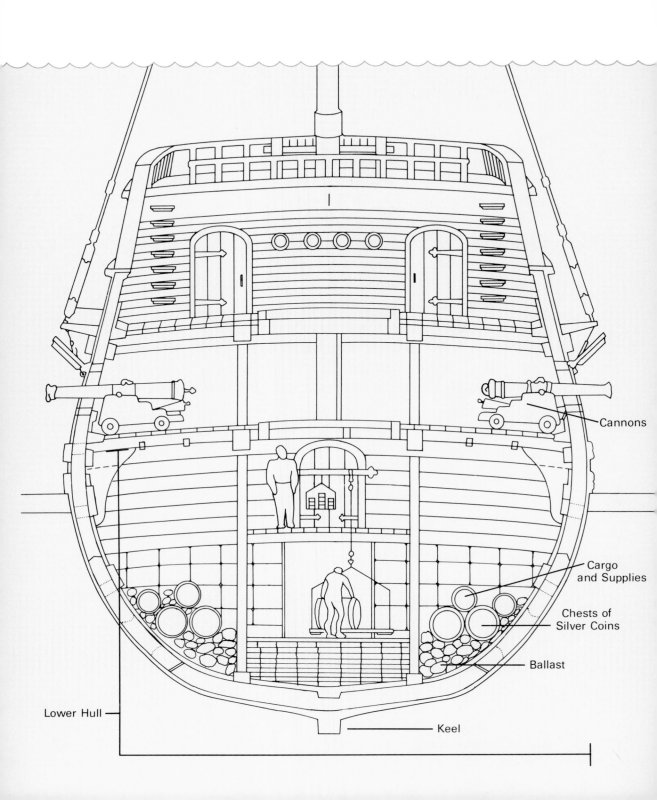

Cannons

Cargo
and Supplies

Chests of
Silver Coins

Ballast

Lower Hull

Keel

The Sinking of the *Atocha*

The *Atocha*, a three-masted flagship weighing 550 tons, sits in the Havana harbor like a great furled ghost. Torches blaze, lighting the way for Indian workers and slaves as they haul huge chests of gold and silver into the ship's storerooms. Sunburned men hoist aboard bales of tobacco, slabs of copper, and bundles of indigo, a blue dye for the cloth weavers in Spain. On the dock, chickens squawk and peck at the wooden slats of their crates. Beside them, sea turtles squirm in pens. The animals will provide fresh meat during the long voyage. Baskets of vegetables and casks of wine and water, enough for many weeks, are also ready to be loaded. Soldiers standing ramrod straight guard chests of gold and piles of silver mined by South American Indians. Other soldiers stand watch beside the gunpowder for the warship's twenty bronze cannons and sixty muskets.

As the first rays of sun light the sky, the passengers arrive. A raven-haired woman, dressed in shiny green silk, steps onto the plank that leads to the *Atocha*. Around her neck hangs a gold cross embedded with emeralds. A priest boards, clutching a string of coral prayer beads, his rosary. Behind him, three children walk alongside their father, a rich merchant returning to his home in Spain. In all, forty-eight members of the Spanish upper class crowd into the cabins of the *Ato-*

This drawing shows a cross-section of the hull of the *Atocha*. Much of the ship's weight was in the lower part of the hull where the silver ingots and ballast were stored (based on a drawing by Bill Muir).

cha's sterncastle. Many of these wealthy men and women carry gold and jewels hidden from the ship's silvermaster and the king's tax officials. Since the valuables do not appear on the ship's manifest, or official list of cargo, their owners will not have to pay the tax on them.

In the final moments of boarding, an officer of the king's army leads 82 soldiers on board. Then, the ship's surgeon runs up the gangway, his bony fingers clutching a leather sack. He carries the herbs and the tools he will

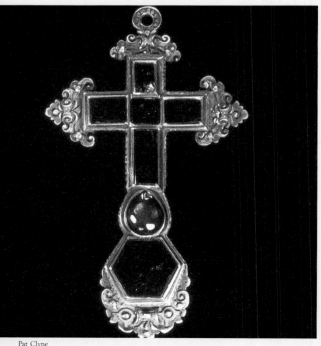

A wealthy passenger on the *Atocha* once carried this beautiful cross.

Pat Clyne

A copy of a page from the *Atocha*'s original manifest.

need to make weary, seasick passengers comfortable. At last, servants, slaves, and sailors join the others on the galleon. The manifest lists 265 persons aboard the ship on this day.

Work stops on the ship while the priest prays for a safe voyage. The fleet must face the dangers of violent storms and attacks by pirates on the high seas. Even though it is September—the height of the hurricane season—the Marquis de Cadereita gives the order to leave. Cannons boom. Trumpets blare. Church bells peal farewell to the fleet. A crowd on the dock cheers as sailors hoist the anchors into the vessels. Twenty-eight ships, white sails billowing, coats-of-arms blazing, sail out of the harbor into the Gulf of Mexico, following the usual trade route to Spain. As the *almiranta*, one of two armed galleons assigned to protect the fleet, the *Atocha* sails at the rear of the fleet.

Two days later, off the coast of Florida, the clouds darken the early morning sky. The sea churns black and violent, pitching the ship to and fro. On deck, sailors run frantically, carrying out the captain's commands: "Reef the sails! Secure the hatches! Man the pumps!" Wind whips at their faces, taking away their breath. Giant waves wash over the bow. The *Atocha* dips into the inky water as the wind drives it toward a craggy coral reef. Suddenly, the sea lifts the mighty ship and smashes

This map shows the route of the *Atocha*'s last voyage. The *Atocha* and *Margarita* sailed in a fleet that stopped at ports in Colombia and Panama to be loaded with silver and gold before sailing on to Havana.

it against the reef. The mast splinters, and the *Atocha* splits into jagged pieces of wood, the sails ripped into ribbons. The roar of the sea muffles the helpless cries of those in the sinking ship.

Within sight of the *Atocha*, its sister ship, the *Santa Margarita*, also founders in the hurricane. In an attempt to save their ship, the *Margarita*'s seamen drop anchors as the vessel crosses a reef. But their efforts are of no use. In the black morning, the ship grounds on a shoal. A soldier clings desperately to the *Margarita*'s bulwarks. Salt stinging his eyes, he watches as the *Atocha* is overcome by the sea. A few hours later, the *Margarita* also breaks apart in the storm. The dazed soldier, Captain de Lugo, floats away from the wreckage on a broken piece of a mast.

All that remains of the two ships are scraps of wood, broken barrels, and shards of planking. Voices of men and women moan against the wind. By afternoon, the wind stops, and the sun beats down on a calm ocean. A passing ship from Jamaica, spying the wreckage bobbing on the water, seeks survivors. Crewmen soon rescue sixty-eight people from the *Margarita*. Captain de Lugo, confused, exhausted, and battered, is pulled from the sea. On board the Jamaican vessel, he weeps. Some of his shipmates are saved, but not many. In time he learns that only five have survived the sinking of the *Atocha*—a seaman, two ship's boys, and two slaves.

Searching for the Lost Treasure

The Jamaican rescue ship, carrying the weary, frightened survivors huddled on its deck, sets sail for Cuba. In port, the Marquis de Cadereita, commander of the king's fleet, paces the dock. His own ship had outrun the deadly hurricane and had returned safely to port in Havana. To his aide, he grumbles, "Eight ships are lost." He touches the bruise on his forehead. The marquis suddenly straightens his back, seeing a foreign ship lowering its sails as it approaches the pier.

A grizzled sailor from the Jamaican ship cups his hands to his mouth and calls out, "Survivors! We need help."

"Bring any officers to me," the marquis says to his aide.

That afternoon, Captain de Lugo sits in a velvet-covered chair facing the marquis. His face flushed, the marquis says, "His majesty needs that gold and silver to pay for the war. Where did the _Atocha_ sink?" He writes furiously as de Lugo recalls the terrible storm.

His visitor gone, the marquis sends for Captain de Vargas, a salvage expert. Hours later, a Cuban officer strides into the commander's chambers. "Captain," says the marquis, "get as many Indian pearl divers as you can find. I am sending Mexican slave divers as well. We must sail right away to the Florida Straits to salvage whatever gold and silver we can." The marquis then commands his servant: "Pack my clothes and heavy boots."

For months, the marquis, Captain de Vargas, and the slave divers and crew camp on a tiny island in the Florida Keys. At four o'clock each morning, the searchers row for many hours in the darkness, arriving by seven o'clock at the place where the ships have sunk.

One by one, each diver lifts a heavy stone from the bottom of the boat, takes a deep breath, and hurls himself headlong into the sea. In the short time he can remain underwater, he must search the turquoise water for a gleam of silver or gold. Weighted down by the stone, he looks for signs of the wreckage. Soon, though, he must surface or drown for lack of air.

After many long days of searching, only a few silver bars are recovered from one of the ships. To make matters worse, gold-seeking Dutch pirates from nearby islands, the Dry Tortugas, hear of the doomed ships. When the pirates sail into the Florida Straits on great warships, the salvors flee as pirate cannons swivel toward them. Defeated, the marquis returns to Cuba.

In Spain, King Philip IV is upset by the news. "There must be someone who can recover my gold."

In 1626, four years after the *Atocha*'s sinking, a clever inventor interests the king in his plan. "Your Majesty," says Francisco Núñez Melián, "I have invented a diving bell that will help me find your treasure ship. Hire me, give me men, and I will restore your riches."

"How can you do this?" the king asks. "My officers have had the world's best divers search for the treasure. They lose their breath or drown before they can find very much."

"I have cast my diving bell in bronze," Melián replies, describing his new invention. "It is large enough to hold two men. Seated on a crossbar, they can view the ocean bottom through a window and breathe air at the same time."

Convinced, the king offers Melián ships, men, and money to begin a salvage expedition. "Write a full report on everything that you see and do," the king demands.

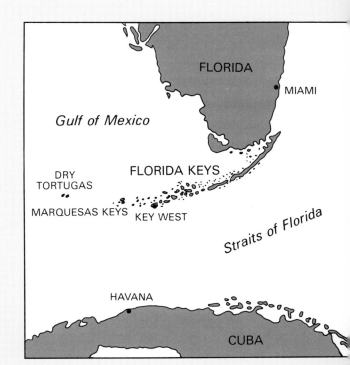

The *Atocha* and the *Margarita* sank near the Marquesas Keys at the end of the chain of islands called the Florida Keys.

Melián's Salvage Attempt

On a hot June day in 1626, Francisco Melián calls his slave divers together. "Whoever finds his Majesty's ship will be a free man this day," he says.

Later, standing at the railing of his ship, Melián peers out at a small salvage boat. The boat drags the diving bell back and forth over the area where the ships sank four years earlier. Inside the bell, a slave, Juan Bañon, breathes the captured air. Studying the sea floor through the glass window of the bell, he spies a galleon lying on its side. He tugs on the rope, which signals to the crew that he wants to stop. The seamen wait as Bañon frees himself from the bell and swims to touch the wreck. From inside the hull, he lifts a bar of silver. Longing for air, he rises, cradling the heavy prize in his arm. To his companions, he shouts, "It is found!" Grinning, Bañon hands the silver bar to his crewmates, and then swims to the side of the larger vessel.

To Francisco Melián, he says, "Señor, you promised my freedom if I found a treasure ship."

"You shall have it," replies Melián. "You are now a free man."

The divers work to exhaustion that day, hauling up more silver, many coins, and two bronze cannons. The ship's pilot runs his fingers over the numbers of a cannon barrel. He looks at the gun list in his hand. "Señor

Melián," he says, "you have found the *Santa Margarita*." For years, Melián and others continue to search for the *Atocha*, but its grave site remains hidden from them.

In his office, Francisco Melián writes a report in great detail. Pressing his ring into the soft wax that seals the scroll, he calls to his servant, "Send this to his Majesty. My work is finished."

For more than three hundred years, the scroll remained in the king's library in Spain, until Eugene Lyon eased the crumbling parchment out of its leather casing.

Science at Work in the Sea

Mel Fisher flipped his diving mask up onto his forehead, pressed his hands to the rails of the diving ladder, and pulled himself aboard his salvage ship.

"Nothing down there," he said to his son. The two stared as a flock of pelicans swooped down to capture baitfish basking near the water's surface. "Somewhere under that water, there's a pile of silver and gold bigger than anyone's ever seen. I can just feel it."

A copy of John Potter's *Treasure Diver's Guide* lay on the galley table. Dog-eared pages described the *Atocha*'s treasure, and the area where it had sunk in the Florida Keys. "I guess today's not the day we find it," Mel said, gazing wistfully at the book.

Mel Fisher had developed his skills as a treasure hunter by locating and salvaging shipwrecks near Florida's east coast. In the late 1960s, he formed a company called Treasure Salvors and moved to the Florida Keys

Matt Bradley

Mel Fisher used salvage vessels such as this Treasure Salvors boat during his long search for the *Atocha*.

to search for the *Atocha*. Yet after four years of exploring around an island in the middle Keys, Fisher had found no trace of the lost ship.

When Eugene Lyon returned to America in 1970, he met with Mel Fisher to examine Melián's scroll, reprinted on microfilm. "Look at this," Lyon said to his friend. "You've been looking for the *Atocha* in the wrong place. You've been searching near a middle Key. Here in Melián's report he says that the ships sank near the last Key. You're at least 100 miles off."

Acting on Lyon's advice, Fisher moved his base of operations to Key West, a town near the end of the chain of islands that form the Florida Keys. From that home port, he headed for the Marquesas Keys. In the Marquesas, powdery white beaches, fringed with sea grasses, slope into turquoise water. Scientists think the Marquesas atoll (a ring of islands surrounding a lagoon) may have been formed by a prehistoric meteorite. Kingfishers and pelicans nest in the red mangroves of the atoll. Glass minnows and baby crabs live securely beneath the tangled roots. In this beautiful area, Mel Fisher continued his search for the Spanish galleon.

In September another roll of microfilm postmarked "Seville" arrived on Lyon's boat. A kind librarian, recalling Lyon's interest, had mailed a copy of a tattered, mouldy letter. It had been written by the marquis who had camped with Captain de Vargas on that salvage expedition long ago. Lyon read the letter carefully. As he translated the old Spanish scroll, his eyes fixed upon a small word, *veste* ("west"). *West*—and Fisher had been searching the waters on the *east* side of the Marquesas Keys. The researcher rushed to tell Mel.

Magnetometers and Mailboxes

For the next several years, Mel Fisher and his crew would search the sea around the atoll, trying to find treasure from the *Atocha*. His salvage ship towed a magnetometer, an instrument used to detect iron underwater, as it criss-crossed the ocean.

Of all the instruments used for treasure hunting, the magnetometer proved the most valuable. Invented by Fay Feild, an electronics expert and friend of Mel Fisher, this device led the divers to thousands of precious finds.

One day, alerted by a strong reading on the magnetometer screen, the divers grabbed their scuba gear and plunged into the water. In a bed of seaweed, near a giant conch shell, rested a coral-covered sword. Gently pushing away a nosy hogfish nibbling at the crusty coral, a diver picked up the once-mighty weapon. The fragile find was later x-rayed. All that remained of the sword was its coral shell and an iron handle almost completely eaten away by seawater. The blade had disappeared.

A Treasure Salvors boat captain watches the magnetometer screen.

Many times, the magnetometer fooled the divers. On one dive, two explorers descended to the sea bottom, only to find empty bombshells littering the barren seascape. The crew soon learned that the area they were exploring had been a U.S. Navy bombing range.

As they searched, the salvage crew constantly faced the same problem: they knew that sands, shifted by currents and tides, had probably covered the *Atocha* and its cargo. To uncover objects hidden beneath the shifting

The boat at the left is equipped with a mailbox, a device invented by Mel Fisher to aid his search for the *Atocha*.

sands, Mel Fisher invented the "mailbox,"* which punched deep holes in the sea floor. Since he needed sturdy boats with powerful propellers to make his mailbox work, Fisher bought two tugs, the *Northwind* and the *Southwind*. He appointed his young sons, Dirk and Kim, as their skippers.

*Mel Fisher's mailbox, a huge, elbow-shaped tube, fits over the propeller, forcing the water downward while the boat is anchored with engines running. The jets of water then swirl away tons of sand.

"The Bank of Spain"

Events in the spring of 1973 caused excitement among the treasure hunters. The old tug *Southwind* was anchored in calm waters while the mailboxes churned under the stern. At a signal from the captain, the divers, seated on the side of the boat, pushed over backwards into the sea. As the first explorer uncurled from her dive, she saw a trail of blackened coins scattered around the crater the mailbox had dug. Bobbing to the surface, she yelled, "Coins! Hundreds of coins!" Several divers rushed to the site and loaded their mesh bags with the silver treasure. One crew member quipped, "This must be the Bank of Spain." All day long, coins clinked as they dropped onto the deck of the *Southwind*.

A month later, Dirk Fisher, suspended at the edge of the underwater storm created by the mailbox, waited impatiently for the sand particles to settle. The sea animals, alerted by the whirr of engines overhead, fled to safety under a nearby coral ledge. In a crater, an unusual round object, half-buried by the thick, muddy sand, stuck out of the sea floor. Dirk pulled out the strange-looking object, turned it over in his hand, and swam up to the boat. Climbing the diving ladder on the side, he proudly waved his prize.

A diver gasped as he touched the find. "This is an astrolabe," he said. He explained to the crew that an

The astrolabe discovered by Dirk Fisher.

astrolabe was used by a ship's pilot in the seventeenth century to observe the position of the stars. The crew looked at one another and wondered. Whose astrolabe was it? Did it belong to the pilot of the *Atocha*?

That summer, the sea offered more than one clue that the *Atocha* was close by. In July, Fisher's fourteen-year-old son Kane, diving around the "Bank of Spain," spied a blackened loaf resting in the sand. Aware of the danger of disturbing moray eels that lurked in the sea rocks, Kane poked carefully at the loaf. It was solid, like silver. The boy struggled to lift the heavy bar. It was too heavy. He rose to the surface and called, "Throw me a rope. I've found something."

Returning to the black object, Kane looped the rope around the find, tightening a slip knot to secure it. On board the *Southwind* a few minutes later, Kane's find was placed in a vat of seawater. Keeping the bar in seawater would prevent any changes from occurring before scientists could examine the find. The crew could see that the bar was silver. Through the blackened coating on its surface, Roman numerals were visible.

"Does anyone remember Roman numerals?" Kane asked. The crew tried to recall old lessons as the *Southwind* steamed back to Key West.

At Treasure Salvors headquarters, Eugene Lyon brushed the black surface of the newest find. The bar was a silver ingot—silver that had been melted and formed into a block so that it could be easily stored and transported. The ingot was clearly engraved with the symbol of the merchant who had shipped it. Beside the shipper's markings were the Roman numerals that translated to 4584.

Lyon searched through the documents sent from the library in Spain. After three days of translating the old Spanish lettering, he announced, "It's here. 4584 is

Pat Clyne

This silver ingot from the *Atocha* bears a tax stamp, a silver fineness number, the owner's identification number, and the date, 1622.

here. That silver bar was loaded onto the *Atocha*." Beside the ancient Roman numerals, a note read: "For payment of tax on a shipment of black slaves unloaded in Cartagena." The king had never received his tax for the selling of human lives.

At last, Fisher and his crew knew that they had found part of the *Atocha*'s treasure. But where was the ship? Like a ghost, it continued to hide from them.

—3—

Following the Atocha's Trail

A rosary of red coral beads joined by fine gold links, a crushed gold poison cup, sparkling gold doubloons, silver spoons and pewter plates—these were some of the treasures recovered by Mel Fisher and his divers near the "Bank of Spain." Like the astrolabe, the new discoveries raised puzzling questions: Who prayed this rosary? What traveler sipped from this gold cup? Who stirred tea with this silver spoon?

Mel Fisher and his staff needed an expert to help them find the answers. They hired an archeologist who could work with them to uncover the secrets the sea was keeping.

As the diving season opened in the spring of 1975, archeologist Duncan Mathewson and the crew anchored their boat over the "Bank of Spain." The archeologist asked the crew to think about the places where they had discovered the coins, the astrolabe, and the silver ingot.

Archeologist Duncan Mathewson.

Two divers drew a map on the back of a paper plate. The mapping of a treasure site had begun.

Mathewson gave the crew underwater archeology lessons daily. Clad in scuba gear, he taught the diving team how to make a grid of plastic pipes over the place where they were digging, the excavation site. Standing at an underwater surveying desk, with a special grease pencil in his hand, he showed some of the divers how to record a survey on a plastic graph.

After diving in search of treasure in the morning, the suntanned divers discussed their day's work on the boat in the afternoon. Mathewson instructed each diver to write down the location of any finds, the depth of the water, and whether the object was found buried in the sand or lying on top of the limestone sea floor.

Angel Fisher, Dirk's wife, drew pictures of the artifacts. Sitting with her sketch pad, she studied the features of the crusty objects. A grapeshot cannonball, made of small iron balls fused together, looked like a bunch of metal grapes. Angel touched the knobby mass, and then sketched it on the clear white pad. A diver once handed her a heavy find. Bits of shell hung onto the blackened crust of an object that appeared to be a candle holder. The cross engraved on its surface hinted that the artifact may once have graced an altar or a shrine in a Spanish home.

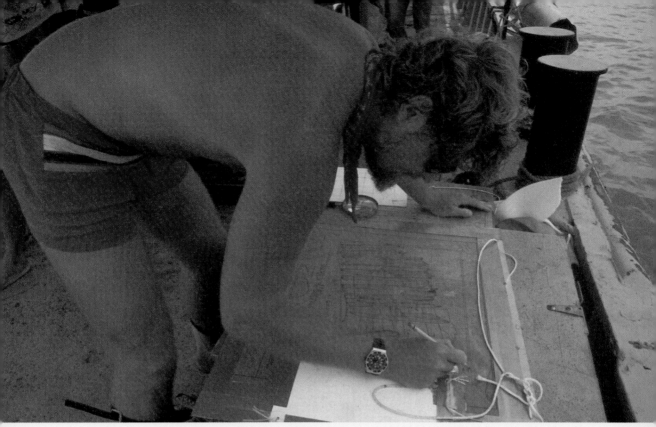

Duncan Mathewson draws a map on "paper" specially made to be used underwater.

Often, Mathewson sat on deck with a large map of the sea unrolled in front of him. On the map, the places where the artifacts had been found were marked. In time, as the archeologist studied the map, he saw a trail emerging. The trail stretched from a galleon anchor, to a pile of silver coins, to an astrolabe, and on to a small stack of silver ingots. Again and again, Mathewson looked at the trail formed by the artifacts. Where was the *Atocha*? he wondered. And where were the cannons that had rolled off the decks of the warship as it tossed about in the hurricane?

The trail of artifacts was confusing. Probably other, later storms had scattered the *Atocha*'s cargo. Mathewson moved his finger along the map, away from the shallow water where they had been searching. He began to believe that the *Atocha* lay in deeper water.

One hot July day, Dirk Fisher stood on the deck of the *Northwind*. Dirk had moved the salvage vessel and its crew to Hawk Channel the night before. Looking out at the buoys, Dirk noticed that the *Northwind* had drifted during the night; her anchors had dragged. He grabbed his scuba tank and mask and swam to check the troublesome anchors. Gliding along the anchor line, accompanied by a school of silver mullet, Dirk reached the sea floor. Suddenly, he froze. There before him on the rocky bottom rested five bronze cannons, poised as they had been for more than 350 years. Dirk rushed to the surface and screamed at the crew on the *Northwind*. In terror, Angel and the others remembered the sharks that prowled these waters. But no shark had startled Dirk. "The cannons," he yelled. "I've found the cannons. Bring the boat over here."

For the next ten minutes, Dirk tread water in the same spot. He wanted to be certain that the cannons would not disappear while the *Northwind* moved.

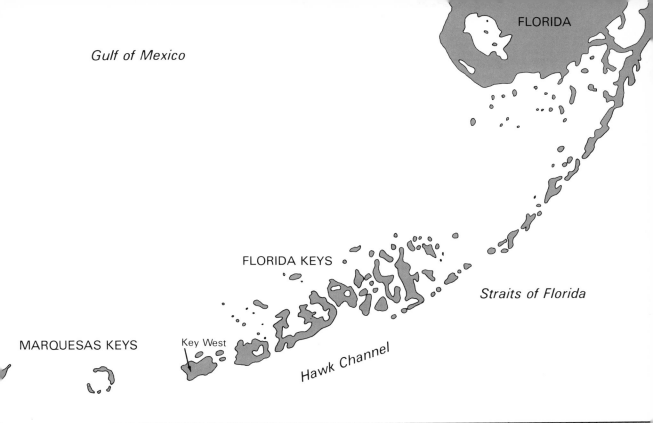

Gulf of Mexico

FLORIDA

FLORIDA KEYS

Straits of Florida

MARQUESAS KEYS

Key West

Hawk Channel

This map shows the Florida Keys and the area around the Marquesas Keys where the Treasure Salvors divers searched for the *Atocha*.

While white-capped waves rose in tiny peaks over Hawk Channel, the winches on board the salvage boat creaked. Straining on the pulleys, a massive cannon barrel soon emerged from the sea. The crowd of divers cheered at the sight of the magnificent gun. As the cannon was raised higher, a diver pointed at the barrel. "Look," he said, "the underside is worn away." Later, when the divers who had recovered the cannon were back on board, one of them said, "As we started to tie

Pat Clyne

Kim Fisher helps guide a cannon on the deck of a Treasure Salvors boat.

up the cannon, a giant turtle slipped out from underneath. It looks like we broke up a turtles' nest."

Mel Fisher examined the cannon. "I think turtles must have been nesting under that gun for centuries. Probably, over hundreds of years, as they crawled in and out, their flippers wore away the metal."

The turtles had worn away the cannon's underbelly; the sea had worn away its identifying marks. Although the crew felt sure that this cannon had fallen from the

Atocha's deck, they had no way to prove it.

The second cannon that was hoisted up that day brought another loud cheer from the crew. Found buried in the sand, this majestic gun had been preserved against saltwater damage. As one diver touched the sculptured dolphins perched on the cannon tube, another diver scraped away greenish silt, revealing Roman numerals clearly etched into the barrel.

Mathewson reached for his briefcase and took out the *Atocha*'s gun list. On parchment, a Spanish scribe had listed the ship's cannons, their weights, and the numbers stamped on them at the foundry where they were made. "It's here," he said quietly. "This cannon once protected the *Atocha*."

Tragedy on the *Northwind*

A few nights later, the lanterns burned brightly on the *Northwind* in Hawk Channel. The crew, joined by Angel's eleven-year-old brother, sang "Happy Birthday" to Angel, and celebrated the discovery of the cannons. Their laughter echoed over the lonely ocean until the lanterns were snuffed out that night. As the crew slept, a slowly leaking valve suddenly burst. Water gushed into the bilge of the old tug. In the darkness, the boat listed to its side quietly, and in a moment the *Northwind* turned upside down in the water.

Several members of the crew, startled from sleep, swam from the vessel. Clinging to the keel in terror, one diver grabbed an uninflated raft that floated by. He put his lips to the plastic nozzle and breathed out short puffs of air to inflate the raft. "Get on," he screamed to Angel's brother. Seconds later, the *Northwind* sank.

At dawn, the numbed survivors, huddled near the raft, saw a white boat approaching through the mist—a Treasure Salvors boat. All but three of the divers had escaped the sinking tug. Angel and Dirk Fisher and another diver had drowned.

The tragedy on the *Northwind* shocked and saddened Mel Fisher. He had lost his son and daughter-in-law and their friend. After the accident, Fisher wanted to give up the search for the *Atocha*. Yet his grieving crew and family would not let him quit. Dirk had found the cannons; the search for the *Atocha* would carry on the dream shared by him and the rest of the Treasure Salvors crew.

Staying on Course

After their comrades' deaths, the crew ended their search for 1975. They came back the next year, determined to find the *Atocha*. For five years, the Treasure Salvors crew mapped the ocean around the Marquesas atoll.

Their course was guided by operators who worked on theodolite towers set up above the water. The theo-

Perched high above the water, theodolite operator Charles Clyne prepares his station for a long day on the search site.

dolite, a kind of telescope, had long been used by surveyors to measure angles. From the two theodolite towers, the operators observed the path of the salvage vessel. They marked the boat's course on a chart. Watching the vessel as it roamed the sea lanes, the tower operators radioed the captain if he veered off course.

The methods for tracking ships improved after inventions such as the theodolite tower, but the sea offered only clues to the treasure seekers. As the explorers hunted for the lost ship, they found scattered artifacts—gold coins minted before 1622, barrel hoops, and a marked gold bar.

The gold bar was marked with the royal seal of Philip IV, the sixteen-year-old king who ruled Spain in 1622. Below the seal, on the right-hand side, the gold bar bore a strange "bite." The archeologist knew that the "bite" was the work of an assayer, who kept a chunk of every gold bar to test for the purity of the metal. The owner of the gold bar had paid a tax to the king based on the weight and purity of the gold. Other mysterious symbols were engraved on the bar, marks that no one could explain.

In spite of some exciting and valuable finds, the money to pay for the expensive salvage operations was almost all spent. Some of the divers quit because there was no money to pay them. Others wanted to continue

Don Kinkaid

These gold bars show the Spanish assayer's "bite."

the search. Packing peanut butter and jelly sandwiches for lunch, the determined treasure hunters set out daily to find the *Atocha*. Like Mel Fisher, they believed it was just a matter of time before the vast treasure was found.

Fisher carefully studied the maps and charts. Again, he examined de Lugo's account of the sinking of the ships in the hurricane. He reread the salvage reports of de Vargas and Melián. The seventeenth-century searchers had recorded the location of the *Santa Margarita*'s sinking, but the exact resting place of the ship was not marked. Perhaps the king had not wanted an exact record of the location. Enemies and pirates might have killed for the chance to recover the king's gold and silver.

The *Margarita* had sunk within sight of the *Atocha*. Of that much, Fisher was sure. He decided to hire another salvage operator, Captain J., to help him find that galleon. If it could be found, he hoped the trail to the *Atocha* would be clear. Fisher instructed one of his divers, R. D. LeClair, to go with Captain J. and to call Treasure Salvors if the new crew found any sign of the *Margarita*.

A Tale of Pirates

Captain J. piloted his boat into the shallow waters close to the coral reef. "I'm getting a strong signal from the magnetometer," he said to LeClair. A crew member pulled on scuba gear and slipped beneath the shimmering surface to investigate. Within minutes, the diver reappeared alongside the boat. "Gold," he gasped, and dived again to the bottom. The rest of the crew joined him, feverishly exploring the sea floor.

By afternoon, gold flashed in the sunlight on deck. In spite of centuries in the sea, the gold still gleamed like new. Unlike other metals, the gold had resisted the corroding effects of seawater. And marine life, such as barnacles, had not attached themselves to this precious metal.

Captain J. grabbed the wheel and headed for Key West. Soon, he eased the boat into the harbor, cut the engines, and dropped anchor. LeClair wondered why they were not pulling up to the pier. He stepped into the cabin to radio Mel about the gold. "Don't touch that radio," Captain J. warned LeClair. Stunned by Captain J.'s threat, LeClair watched as he strapped a revolver around his waist. Then, Captain J. radioed a secret signal to his pirate friends that he had found gold and would meet them on a nearby island.

At that moment, a photographer from Treasure Salvors, who was walking along the dock, noticed Captain J.'s boat moored in the harbor. Puzzled, he watched as the vessel raced out toward the channel. The photographer ran to the Treasure Salvors office to tell Mel Fisher.

That night, Captain J. met with a U.S. marshal to claim the gold for himself. He told the marshal that he had found the gold on the site of an unclaimed shipwreck.

Meanwhile, Mel Fisher called his lawyer. "I hired Captain J. to work for me," said Fisher, "and I have a right to the gold on that shipwreck site."

To settle the dispute, the two men took their case to the Florida courts. A judge ordered Captain J. to give the gold back to Mel Fisher because Captain J. had broken his contract.

Examining the precious bars in their office, Fisher and his team knew from the markings that the gold bars had been loaded onto the *Margarita*. Treasure from the *Atocha*'s sister ship had been found by a pirate!

Salvaging the *Margarita*

In the spring of 1980, Treasure Salvors vessels combed the site where Captain J. had recovered the gold bars. Kane Fisher, swimming around the search area, spotted a stack of silver ingots. He swam closer. Next to the ingots was a strange-looking mass. He ran his hand over the bumpy surface. Molded into the shape of the wooden chest that once held them, thousands of silver coins had been fused together by the effects of seawater. Over the years, seaworms had devoured the oak boards of the treasure chest, leaving only the silver contents.

Kane's discovery attracted other divers to the site. The team then made a startling discovery. Half-buried under a pile of heavy stones, ribs of wood stuck out from the sand. The divers could see that the ribs formed a shape. By the oval pattern of the planking, they knew that they were looking at the skeleton of a ship. That afternoon the noisy crew docked in Key West. When Eugene Lyon heard their news, he quickly pulled out the manifests—the official cargo records—of the old ships. Lyon studied the markings on the silver ingots. On the *Margarita*'s manifest, he noted the same markings. The ship that had sunk on the same night as the *Atocha* had been found. Surprisingly, the ship's lower hull had not been completely destroyed by the sea.

Duncan Mathewson wondered why the hull had not been devoured by shipworms. On a dive, he studied the ship's timbers. He concluded that the ship had been buried and preserved by sand until very recently. The strong ocean currents must have moved away the sand, leaving the hull exposed for the twentieth-century treasure hunters.

All during the summer of 1980, Mel Fisher's crew worked at the site of the *Margarita*. A crew member, snorkeling on the surface of the water one morning, glimpsed the glint of gold on the white bedrock. Beneath him, nine gold bars and eight gold chains sparkled in the blue water. That afternoon the tired divers exchanged their scuba gear for gold chains and wore the latest treasure back to Key West.

The finding of the *Margarita*'s treasure renewed the spirit of adventure for the crew. From the sea, they gathered riches unlike any they had ever seen. One diver

plucked from the seabed a plate of solid gold. He examined the engraved flowers covering the plate, the work of an ancient goldsmith. A jeweler, inspecting the plate later, marveled at the eight-inch (twenty-centimeter) circle of perfect gold. "This plate is priceless," he said.

A solid gold bosun's whistle that had once hung on the neck of one of the *Margarita*'s officers was recovered by another diver. On board with his find, the diver blew into the whistle, and its clear, shrill tone silenced the crew. The chill of the sound recalled a night when the bosun had signaled over the howling winds to the desperate crew that hung onto the ship's tattered riggings.

In all, treasure worth $20 million was recovered from the *Santa Margarita*. Mel Fisher and his company now had enough money to continue their hunt for the *Atocha*.

Mel Fisher examines a solid gold plate just found by a Treasure Salvors diver.

–4–

Put Away
the Charts

On the wall behind Mel Fisher's desk hung a map studded with pins showing the places where each artifact from the *Atocha* had been found. Like a beaded necklace, the colored pins formed a linked chain on the blue paper. Yet nowhere on the map was there a bead for the galleon's large ballast stones. In the seventeenth century, no large ship went to sea without the heavy weighted stones that balanced its lower hull.

Like seafaring detectives, Mel Fisher, Eugene Lyon, and Duncan Mathewson reviewed the story of the *Atocha*, seeking a clue that would lead them to the sunken ship's hiding place. They all knew that on a September day in 1622, Indian slaves carried a fortune in silver into the ship's dark, airless lower hull. On each side of the ballast stones, the slaves stacked about fifty tons of silver for delivery to Cadiz, Spain.

While shipworms devour wood, no sea creature can

A diver holds a clump of silver coins.

make a meal of a ballast stone. Wherever the large stones that balanced the *Atocha* rested on the seabed, tons of silver could not be far away. Mathewson often said, "Show me ballast and I'll show you treasure."

For five years following the discovery of the *Margarita* in 1980, Fisher's crew searched in vain for the *Atocha*. Divers surveyed the sea bottom, probing hills of coral in their search for the ballast pile that guarded the galleon's greatest treasures.

The ship's manifest listed more than 1,000 silver ingots and more than 100 gold bars. All of these, along with treasure chests brimming with emeralds and silver coins of the wealthy passengers, vanished with the *Atocha*. Mel Fisher knew that these valuables were worth hundreds of millions of dollars—a hidden pile of treasure he called the "mother lode." On Memorial Day in 1985, a call from the *Dauntless* crew renewed his hopes that the mother lode would soon be found.

Clues to the Treasure

In the steaming morning after Memorial Day, Mel Fisher wore a t-shirt that proclaimed "Today's the Day!" He hopped into his small motorboat and sped out to Hawk Channel to visit the site where his divers had recently discovered gold chains and silver coins.

Climbing aboard the *Dauntless*, Mel shook hands

Pat Clyne

Mel Fisher celebrates with his crew after divers discovered gold and silver artifacts from the *Atocha* on Memorial Day 1985.

with his crew. "Congratulations! I think today may really be the day we find the mother lode," he said. "Good luck on your dive. And while you're down there, look for the chest of emeralds smuggled aboard that ship." Based on his research, Fisher believed that sailors smuggled hundreds of uncut emeralds onto the *Atocha*.

The first two divers into the water that day were a husband and wife team. Pausing in the quiet, deep water, they watched as the familiar barracuda glided by them.

Scott Nierling

These emeralds, coins, gold chain, and brooch were recovered from the *Atocha*.

The partners cleared away the silt in a pocket formed by the mailbox digging. Fanning the sand aside, the young woman spotted a pile of pebbles. In the dark greenish light of the ocean bottom, she examined one of the stones. Scraping her nail across the surface, she recognized the gritty, glassy texture of an uncut emerald. She held the precious stone out in her hand for her husband to see. Together, the two dug feverishly in the sliding sand. They loaded hundreds of valuable emeralds into their mesh bags before returning to the *Dauntless*.

Breathing hard from excitement, the young woman told the crew, "It looks like Mel was right." She held up the mesh bag she had hauled aboard. Seawater dripped from the netting. "There's more," she said.

Her partner added, "We saw some rocks scattered down there. They look like small ballast stones."

Now the clusters of pins formed an even longer necklace on the blue map behind Mel's desk. The pins showed where the gold, precious stones, and cannons were found. Mel scooped more pins into his palm. Pushing the pins into the map, he marked the sites where emeralds and small ballast stones had been recovered.

Duncan Mathewson had a keen interest in another object found by the Treasure Salvors divers. In his hand he held a chain plate that he thought once supported the wind-filled sails of the *Atocha*. To him, this piece of rigging was as precious as the gold and emeralds that sank with the galleon. Three centuries before, a Spanish sailmaker tied his sails to this piece of rigging. In the violent winds of the hurricane, the chain plate and shreds of the sails had fallen into the sea. Found near the site of the emeralds, this chain plate rigging was a sign that the *Atocha*'s grave could be nearby.

For six weeks, the divers explored the ocean floor where they had recovered the emeralds and ship's rig-

The *Dauntless* at the site where the "mother lode" from the *Atocha* was found.

ging. From the salvage boat, the rugged mailbox punched holes in the seabed. The divers, now trained in archeology, numbered each of the holes on a chart, and then began to examine the holes for artifacts.

The digging yielded a rich harvest. Before long, the divers gathered other pieces of a ship's rigging, called drift pins, elegant silver forks, and hundreds of pieces of eight, blackened by silver oxide. A gentle rubbing on one of the coins revealed the unmistakable seal of the boy king, Philip IV, and the date, 1621. By now the whole crew knew that coins would provide the surest proof of the date of a shipwreck. They worked frantically to find the galleon.

The "Mother Lode"

On July 20, 1985, the magnetometer sent an urgent message. The captain watched as the needle jumped insistently. "Check the sonar," he called to a crew member. The dotted pattern of the sonar confirmed the presence of an unusual formation on the sea floor.

Two divers, Andy and Greg, pushed off the side of the *Dauntless* and slipped under the waves to begin their search. Clearing their ears to relieve the pressure of the increasing depth, they descended to the sea bottom. Suddenly, Greg pointed toward an uneven hill of stones. Thinking that the blurry water might be playing tricks on his eyes, Andy tipped his head back, lifted his mask, and blew bubbles into it to clear the glass. But the pile of stones was real. Instantly, the two divers rushed toward the stone pile.

The seascape before them looked like an ancient ruin. The large rocks formed a crude wall almost as tall as Andy and Greg. Lacy coral sea fans flanked the wall. After Greg touched one of the smooth stones, he flashed the "thumbs up" sign to his partner. The signal told

Andy, in scuba language: "Let's go up." Together, following their bubbles, they climbed the anchor line to the waiting *Dauntless* to tell the captain, Kane Fisher, what they had found.

On hearing the news, Kane shouted, "All right!" The crew yelled questions at Andy and Greg. "How big is the wall?" "Did you see any treasure?"

"Let's get our gear," someone shouted.

Kane picked up the radio transmitter and relayed a secret message to the staff at Treasure Salvors in Key West. "We've just backed up to a five-foot wall of ballast."

At Treasure Salvors, the woman who took Kane's message bolted from her chair and ran to find Mel Fisher. A newspaper reporter, pacing outside the office, waited for news of the treasure. All summer long, Fisher had promised her a big story about the *Atocha*.

"Where's Mel?" echoed through the rooms of the old warehouse. Unaware of the latest news, Mel Fisher was looking at fins and snorkels in a local dive shop.

Meanwhile, Andy and Greg returned to the wall of ballast stones. With his metal detector, Andy surveyed the sea floor near the ballast pile. Suddenly, the instrument screeched. Andy stopped to look ahead. In front of him, beady-eyed lobsters waved their antennae from the cracks in a large mound. The metal detector

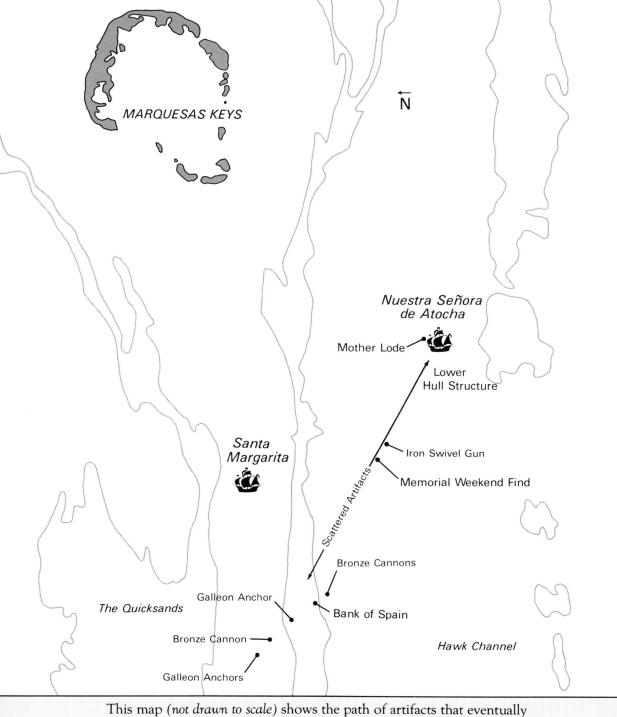

MARQUESAS KEYS

N

Nuestra Señora
de Atocha

Mother Lode

Lower
Hull Structure

Iron Swivel Gun

Memorial Weekend Find

Santa
Margarita

Scattered Artifacts

Bronze Cannons

Galleon Anchor

The Quicksands

Bank of Spain

Bronze Cannon

Hawk Channel

Galleon Anchors

This map (*not drawn to scale*) shows the path of artifacts that eventually led the Treasure Salvors divers to the site of the *Atocha*'s hull. The areas outlined in gray are features of the sea bottom near the Marquesas Keys where divers discovered the wrecks of the *Margarita* and the *Atocha* (based on a drawing by Bill Muir).

screeched louder as Andy approached the mound. He motioned to Greg. The two divers picked at the tiny shells and coral that grew on the mound, as the resident lobsters snapped at them with strong claws. Through their gloved hands, the explorers felt the familiar shapes of silver bars. Both divers grinned behind their masks, and then hugged each other.

Andy was the first to reach the water's surface. Spitting out his mouthpiece, he screamed to the crew of the *Dauntless*, "It's the mother lode! We're sitting on silver bars!"

On board, the divers shouted, hugged, and sang until Kane signaled for a moment's quiet. On the radio to Treasure Salvors, he announced, "Put away the charts; we found the main pile!" The radio operator at Treasure Salvors heard a wild cheer from the crew on the *Dauntless.*

"Drop the buoys," Kane said to the joyful crew. Before the *Dauntless* returned to Key West, the crew waited for another boat to arrive at the site. From this time on, a boat would guard the *Atocha* night and day.

While the staff celebrated at the Treasure Salvors office, the local radio station broadcasted the news that everyone in Key West had been waiting to hear. Wearing a flowered shirt, shorts, and flip flops, Mel Fisher strolled down the main street of Key West. From a shop doorway shaded by a banyan tree, a young man in swim trunks called, "Way to go, Mel." From a passing car, a girl yelled, "Mel, you did it."

Mel quickened his step. As he rushed toward Treasure Salvors, townspeople patted him on the back, saying, "Congratulations!" A radio blared the local news from a car parked at the curb. "If anybody sees Mel Fisher, tell him he found the big pile." The next day the newspaper headline read, "*Atocha* Mother Lode at Last."

—5—

The End
of the Quest

While Treasure Salvors celebrated its victory, Hurricane Bob lashed across the Florida Keys. Palm trees along the shore bent over from the force of the fierce wind. The crew, landlocked for two days, watched as white veins of lightning streaked across the dark sky. Twenty-foot (six-meter) swells crashed over the lone boat stationed above the *Atocha*, guarding the newly found treasure. On the third day, the sun burst through the clouds, the driving winds died down, and the sea grew calmer.

Murky water created by the storm did not slow down the excited diving team that jumped into the sea that day. Bright orange buoys floating on the surface marked the location of the shipwreck. Following the buoy lines down to the cinder blocks that secured them, Andy and Greg led the divers to the stack of silver discovered just days before. The divers stared in amazement. Tangled fishing line wrapped the mound of ingots

Diver Greg Wareham measures a chest of silver coins on board the *Dauntless*.

in a nylon web. For many years fishermen had cast their lines onto this huge silver reef. Thinking they had snagged a coral ledge, they had cut the fishing lines.

Andy pulled his knife from a holder fastened around his leg and cut the web of fishing line. The divers began to uncover some of the hundreds of heavy silver bars. They struggled to load the 100-pound (45.4-kilogram) ingots into plastic milk crates. Pulling on a cord attached to a winch on the salvage vessel, a diver signaled when an ingot was ready to be hoisted into the boat. After a few hours, the captain had to halt the salvage operation for the day. The weight of the ingots caused the boat's stern to sag dangerously low in the water.

Excited by the great riches of the *Atocha*, the divers eagerly raced to bring silver to the waiting boats. The boats competed to see which one could haul the most silver aboard.

Duncan Mathewson was worried. He knew that the hull of the *Atocha* might be under the silver reef, and that the site should be explored carefully. Trying to calm the excited divers, he told them: "The treasure of the ship is not just in gold and silver; the ship is a time capsule. Much can be learned about life on board a seventeenth-century ship if the *Atocha* is carefully excavated. The whole world is watching us. Do the best job you possibly can."

For the excavation of the majestic ship that had so long hidden from them, Mel Fisher called in more archeologists. All agreed that the mailbox was too powerful for the job of uncovering the parts of the ship. Its churning might disturb, break, or even destroy precious artifacts.

Mel Fisher suggested using another of his inventions for this very special project. The airlift would gently clear mud off the site by means of long hoses.

The team dragged the airlift hoses to the seabed to search for the *Atocha*'s timbers beneath the place where the silver reef and ballast stones were discovered. Patiently, the divers sifted the silt and mud. They felt the steady vibration of the hoses in their hands as the airlift gently blew away layer after layer of sand. At last a diver pointed excitedly to a curved piece of wooden planking. It was a part of the *Atocha*, preserved from the destruction of the salty sea.

An Archeological Treasure

For days, the divers worked to uncover the *Atocha*. Clouds of sand particles hid the divers as they used the airlift to uncover the remains of the sunken ship. When they finished, the lower hull of the *Atocha* stretched beneath them. On the galleon's wooden ribs rested another fortune in treasure.

On the day following the discovery of the ship's

hull, the pulleys on board the salvage vessel worked steadily as the divers raised the long-lost cargo out of the sea. The crew watched in wonder as eight wooden treasure chests, long buried beneath the sand, were lowered onto the deck. The seawater had changed the hard wood into a substance that felt like soft cardboard. When the curious crew pried open the lid of one chest, gold bars glinted in the sunlight! Then another lid was raised— thousands of silver pieces of eight filled the chest!

To record the ship's archeological treasure, divers set up a grid over the *Atocha*. Arms filled with plastic pipes, a team descended to the sea floor and fitted the pieces of pipe together. Assembled, the grid looked like a giant tic-tac-toe board. Once the divers had it in place, they began their digging, recalling Mathewson's directions: "Look carefully into each block of the grid. Make sure that when you find something, you record that object and where you found it." From the divers' notes, Mathewson and other archeologists hired by Mel Fisher could determine what happened when the *Atocha* sank.

Photographers followed the divers as they explored the sandy site of the shipwreck. One photographer, his camera clicking continuously, took several pictures of each artifact as it was uncovered. Another took hundreds of photographs of the timbers of the great ship's hull. Later, in his laboratory, he put the pictures

Divers use an airlift—an underwater vacuum cleaner—to remove layers of sand, silt, and light mud from the lower hull of the *Atocha*.

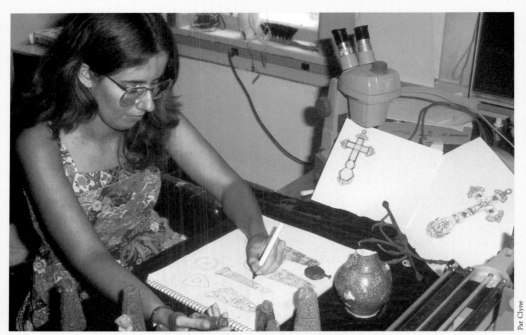

An artist sketches artifacts recovered from the *Atocha*.

together like a jigsaw puzzle and created a photomosaic for marine archeologists (scientists who study shipwrecks and other human remains in the sea) and historians to study.

Later, at Treasure Salvors, an artist studied the artifacts carefully. Her keen eye noticed things the camera might have missed. She could see the tiny holes where quill pens once fit into an inkstand the divers had discovered on the ship.

"Perhaps the captain of the *Atocha* used this ink-stand when he wrote his log," the artist said to a co-worker. He agreed, adding that the captain must have had a sand shaker to help dry the ink. Several days later, the divers found such a sand shaker and brought it to the artist. She drew a pen and ink sketch of the valuable artifact.

During the next month, a team of archeologists swam over the *Atocha*'s hull, measuring and numbering each timber. A surveyor marked the exact position of each part of the ship. These scientists were so involved in their work that they often had to be reminded to check their air supply. They carried miniature tanks of air, called pony bottles, in case of emergency.

As the salvage work continued, an archeologist watched at all times to record the location of each find on an underwater slate. From a square on the grid, a young diver brushed the sand away from a gold ingot. Even in the cloudy water that surrounded the busy site, other divers could see the sparkle of gold, unchanged by centuries in the sea.

For the rest of the 1985 summer diving season, Treasure Salvors divers continued to uncover treasure—the greatest undersea treasure ever recovered from a shipwreck. Other boats at the site helped protect the *Atocha* from would-be pirates. Reporters and photographers

Pat Clyne

A diver examines a new discovery from one of the squares of the grid over the hull of the *Atocha*.

from national newspapers and magazines observed each find on board boats moored at the site. They wrote articles and took pictures as the busy divers climbed the diving ladder with their treasures.

One morning a diver came up the ladder holding a few small objects crusted with tiny coral shells. A crewmate plunged the objects into a fiberglass tank filled with seawater. To the reporters, she explained, "Exposure to the air will destroy many of these objects until they are treated in the lab; so, we put them into salt water to keep them safe until they are examined."

"Can you tell what those objects are?" a reporter asked.

A member of the archeology team examined the objects resting in the tank. "These may be the surgeon's tools," he said. "In the seventeenth century, the surgeon not only treated the patients; he was their pharmacist, too. He ground up the herbs in that mortar with that pestle to make medicine for seasickness, dysentery, or fevers."

Another reporter, pointing to the mortar and pestle, asked, "How will you remove the coral?"

"After we x-ray the objects to see whether they are sturdy, we dip them in an acid bath that dissolves the coral," the archeologist explained. "Sometimes the X ray shows that only the coral covering remains, and the object inside has rusted away."

Understanding the Past

The salvage boat, heavy with treasure, returned each day to Treasure Salvors in Key West. Here, the laboratory on the second floor was the center of much activity. In white coats, skilled workers sorted, cleaned, and preserved the treasure.

As the *Atocha*'s many silver coins were delivered to

Joe Bereswill

In the laboratory, a researcher cleans silver coins, called cobs.

the laboratory, the workers removed them carefully from their water-filled containers. Researchers, with hands blackened by silver oxide, clipped individual coins called cobs* onto wires. Rows upon rows of Spanish pieces of eight and four were then dipped into a vat filled with a special solution. A worker flipped a switch, send-

*Cobs are not perfectly rounded like modern coins, because they were cut from an uneven silver rod. After the coins were cut, a metalworker hammered markings and dates on them.

ing a weak electric current through the solution. The current caused the coral and the black film to dissolve from the coins.

Other researchers sorted the cleaned coins into heaps. Using a computer, they kept a detailed list of every piece of silver brought to the laboratory. Finally, each coin was photographed.

Upstairs at Treasure Salvors, a marine archeologist lifted boxes of broken plates and jars onto a table. Blue ceramic pieces needed to be identified and fitted together, if possible. In the laboratory, thousands of shards of pottery filled other cardboard boxes. The archeologist instructed the college student volunteers: "Separate these pieces. Divide them into clay, pottery, and ceramic. Then we'll work on fitting the pieces together."

Then he left the volunteers to work on another project. The marine archeologist tested uncleaned pieces of olive jars to find out what the jars held when they were loaded onto the *Atocha*. After scraping away the crust on one of the jars, he dropped samples of the dried-up particles into a special chemical solution. In time, using a high-powered microscope, he examined the sample and identified particles of wine. From his studies, much would be learned about the food and drink set aside for the *Atocha*'s passengers during their long voyage across the Atlantic Ocean.

Whenever he made a discovery, the marine archeologist discussed his findings with an archeologist who had studied the everyday customs and eating habits in the seventeenth century. The scientist then reached for the journal he kept on his desk. He wrote about life aboard a ship three hundred and fifty years ago.

In another part of the laboratory, an artist and a historian examined pictures of seventeenth-century nobles in an old book. A Spanish princess, dressed in dark velvet, caught their interest. "Here it is," said the historian, pointing to the beautiful gold and pearl necklace worn by the noblewoman.

The artist touched the broken pieces of jewelry lying on the table. Looking at the picture, she fitted together two chunks of gold. Holes in the pieces hinted that they may once have been filled with pearls and rubies. Studying every detail of the picture, the artist drew the necklace on her sketch pad. Aided by her drawings, a jewelry expert restored the precious necklace to its original beauty and form.

The jewelry expert also restored many pendants found with the *Atocha*. Seagoing travelers usually wore pendants around their necks. Filled with sweet-scented musk or fragrant ambergris, these pendants, or pomanders, masked some of the strong smells coming from other unwashed passengers.

A laboratory worker studies a large pottery jar from the *Atocha*.

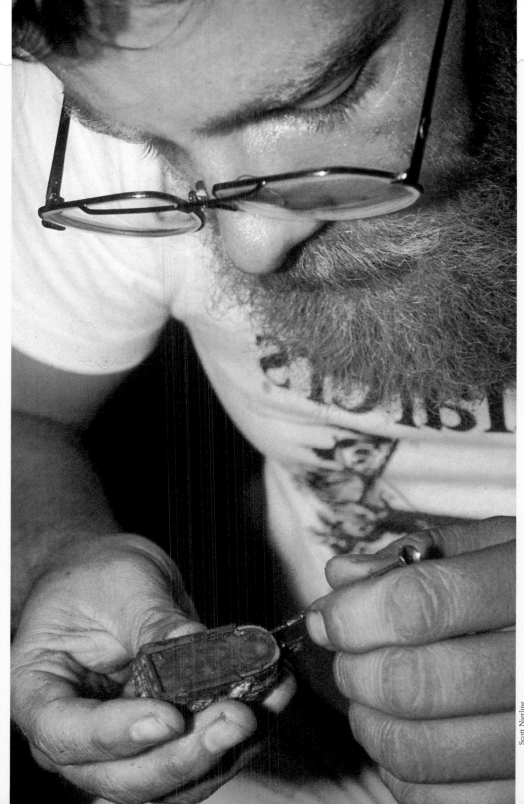

The laboratory team learned about the superstitions of the *Atocha* travelers through the possessions they carried on board. When a cup of crushed gold was brought into the laboratory, a historian searched the library for pictures of such a drinking vessel. His research revealed that the crushed cup was called a "poison cup." A wealthy, high-ranking passenger on the *Atocha*, fearful for his life, probably carried the poison cup with him.

Etched lions, rabbits, and dragons decorated the outside rim of the cup. In the well of the cup was a place for the bezoar stone. The ancient traveler believed that by putting the bezoar stone—taken from the stomach of a goat or llama—in the bottom of his cup as he drank, he would be protected from harm. He thought the bezoar stone would absorb poison, such as arsenic, from his drink.

From the crusty artifacts and muddy finds of the *Atocha*, the archeologists were able to learn much about seventeenth-century life in the New World. Long after the diving season ended in 1985, the laboratory's work continued. When the divers finally covered the ship's remains with large sheets of plastic weighted down by sand, the scientific excavation of the *Atocha* had just begun.

A conservator pries open a tiny jewel box. He repairs and restores artifacts from the *Atocha* so that they can be viewed in their original form.

-6-

A Treasure from the Sea

Beneath the puffs of white clouds that drifted lazily across the pale blue sky of Key West stood an old, salty, weatherbeaten warehouse. The warehouse, once a U.S. Navy building, was now the Treasure Salvors Museum. Tourists in tank tops, shorts, and sandals arrived daily to view the fantastic treasure of the *Atocha*.

As visitors entered the museum, they passed a centuries-old cannon. Inside the museum, a stack of silver ingots rose in a crooked mound from the floor. Light gleamed from glass cases that displayed thick gold chains, emerald jewels, and bars of solid gold.

A young girl paused in front of a lighted case that held a slim gold ring laced with emeralds. She read a card beside the case that told the story of the ring. The card explained that in 1622, a Spanish woman, probably a wealthy woman, had set out on a journey aboard the *Atocha*. Perhaps she wore this magnificent ring on her

At the Treasure Salvors Museum, Mel Fisher and a friend look at stacks of silver and gold chains and bars.

slender finger, or carried it in a silver box. For more than three centuries, the ring had rested on the bottom of the sea. The young girl moved away quietly, thinking about the story of the woman aboard the *Atocha*.

The Raising of the *Atocha*

The hushed tones of the museum were not at all like the lively voices of Mel Fisher and his Treasure Salvors staff upstairs. They discussed what to do with the timbers of the *Atocha*'s hull. For centuries the galleon had rested in the seabed, protected by a 4-foot (1.2-meter) layer of sand. Since the hull had been uncovered, the staff had to decide how to protect it.

To the archeologists, the hull was the greatest treasure of the *Atocha*—more precious than gold, silver, or jewels. The scientists debated whether to bring the entire hull to the surface, or to leave it on the sea floor.

"If we raise the timbers, the wood will shrink and crumble. We should leave the ship where it is," argued one archeologist.

Another archeologist had a different opinion. "If we leave the hull of the *Atocha* where it is, the ship will eventually decay and disappear forever. Shipworms and sea salt will ruin the hull now that it is unburied. If we bring the timbers up, we can study them and perhaps preserve them from further damage."

After listening to the arguments, Mel Fisher decided to raise the *Atocha* and to donate the hull to the Florida Keys Community College. The college offered to put the precious timbers into a protected saltwater lagoon, 38 feet (11.6 meters) deep. The special silt of the lagoon would prevent shipworms from destroying the wood.

Before the pieces of the *Atocha* were moved, one of the archeologists, Corey Malcom, put on his diving gear and descended to the ocean floor to examine the hull. He noticed the broken planking where the *Atocha* crashed into the reef during the hurricane. Probing the planking, he found caked mud wedged between the boards. Malcom scraped mud samples into several plastic bags and left shortly before a crew of U.S. Navy divers began to raise the ship's hull.

Divers gently guided pieces of the ship, tagged with big red numbers, out of the ocean. Sturdy chains held the 1,600-pound (727-kilogram) timbers as they were lifted onto a waiting U.S. Navy ship. In a few weeks, the Navy vessel salvaged forty mahogany timbers from the deep water. Later, the 20-foot (6.1-meter) pieces of wood were loaded onto a barge that could travel through the shallow water to the lagoon next to the college.

An excited crowd greeted the barge at Key West Community College, where the timbers were gently lowered into the lagoon. Already the college was design-

Pat Clyne

Divers raise and measure one of the timbers from the *Atocha*.

ing an original program in underwater archeology. Educators planned to invite middle school children and their teachers to dive into the lagoon and to touch the *Atocha*.

New Life from Ancient Seeds
When the timbers arrived, Corey Malcom was already hard at work in the Treasure Salvors laboratory. He and his assistants took the mud from the plastic bags and emptied it into fresh water. Then they sifted the muddy

Joe Bereswill

A timber from the *Atocha* is hoisted aboard the waiting U.S. Navy ship.

water through a screen. Sediment remained on the screen after the water had flowed through.

Next Malcom emptied the sediment into a container of sugar water, which allowed the particles in the mud to separate. For three months, the staff worked to continue separating the particles.

Each day the researchers made new discoveries. The fossilized bodies of insects that had fed on the ship's food supplies floated among the particles. Beans, thorns, and leaf fragments rose to the surface of the sugar water—and hundreds of tiny seeds.

Using a dental pick, Malcom separated the seeds. Placing the seeds on a slide, he studied them under a microscope. The archeologist recognized grape seeds. Other seeds were mysterious; he did not know what they were. Like a gardener, he placed the seeds in fresh water to see if they would sprout.

One morning Malcom arrived at the laboratory and checked his experiment. Tiny green shoots had sprouted from the seeds. The excited archeologist then planted the shoots in soil. In time, the sprouts grew into full-sized plants. From his books, the scientist identified the plant as "beggar's tick," a weed that grows everywhere on Caribbean islands. The hardy seeds had survived more than three centuries in the sea, protected by a covering of thick, dried mud.

Newspapers carried the story of the ancient seeds that sprouted after 350 years in the sea. Corey Malcom wondered how the seeds were carried onto the ship. Did a slave who helped to shovel the ballast stones into the galleon's lower hull bring the seeds in on his clothing?

Each new discovery raises such questions, and the scientists keep searching for answers. They expect to explore the mysteries of the *Atocha* for at least ten more years.

Corey Malcom observes a sprout from a seed he recovered from the *Atocha*.

Investors in the *Atocha*

Not all of the treasure of the *Atocha* is stored at the Treasure Salvors Museum. Much of the treasure belongs to the more than one thousand people who gave Mel Fisher the money he needed during the sixteen-year hunt for the *Atocha*. Called investors, these people risked their money because they believed Mel Fisher and his crew would find the enormous treasure and make them rich.

When the *Atocha* was found, the crew recovered approximately 400,000 items. Each individual coin and musket ball, as well as every emerald and gold bar, was labeled with a special identification tag. The information on the tag, along with a digital picture of each piece of treasure, was stored in a computer. The computer then gave "points" to each item according to its value. For example, a small emerald was given 2 points, while a large emerald was given 20,000 points. A vice-president of Treasure Salvors said, "The $1,000 investor received approximately 328 points of treasure."

The inventory, or list of articles recovered from the sea, was 2,700 pages long. When the time came for the division of the treasure in October 1986, the computer again went to work. The investors were to be paid in treasure, rather than in cash. For two and a half days, the Treasure Salvors office staff heard the steady click of the

Some of the *Atocha* treasure on display at Treasure Salvors Museum.

printer running out pages filled with the names of the investors and their share of the treasure.

At the end of the computer division, investors were asked to come to Key West to pick up their valuables. Many investors went to Key West and held a grand celebration. Other investors sent armed guards to bring back their treasure. One man, Melvin Joseph of Delaware, received hundreds of pieces of treasure in silver, gold, and jewels. He decided to give most of the treasure to a college in his hometown. Now that college, the Delaware Technical and Community College in Georgetown, Delaware, has built a special museum to hold the *Atocha* treasure.

Some of the treasure was auctioned off in Las Vegas in September 1987. The coral rosary sold for $375,000. One gold chain fetched $300,000.

Though the largest collections of artifacts are displayed in the museums in Florida and in Delaware, people throughout the United States hold pieces of the *Atocha*'s treasure. More treasure is still being brought up from the sea. After hundreds of years, the story of the lost treasure galleon continues.

A Love of Adventure

Mel Fisher often leaves the Treasure Salvors offices to return to the sea. He has sold the company, and now has more time to spend doing what he enjoys the most—treasure hunting. Although his great quest for the *Nuestra Señora de Atocha* has ended, his love of adventure remains as strong as ever.

On warm summer days, standing on the deck of a shiny boat, he seizes the mask and fins from a green plastic pail. Hitching a scuba tank over his back, buckling the gear and weight belts securely, he prepares to take a giant step off the top rung of the diving ladder.

Once again, Mel Fisher explores the cool green waters of the sea he knows so well.

The briny foam of the ocean waves washes the beaches of the Florida Keys. Beyond the breakers, buried in watery graves, hundreds, perhaps thousands, of wrecked ships have yet to be discovered. In their holds, millions of dollars worth of gold, silver, and jewels rest. As long as there are treasure hunters like Mel Fisher, these sunken ships will not be forgotten.

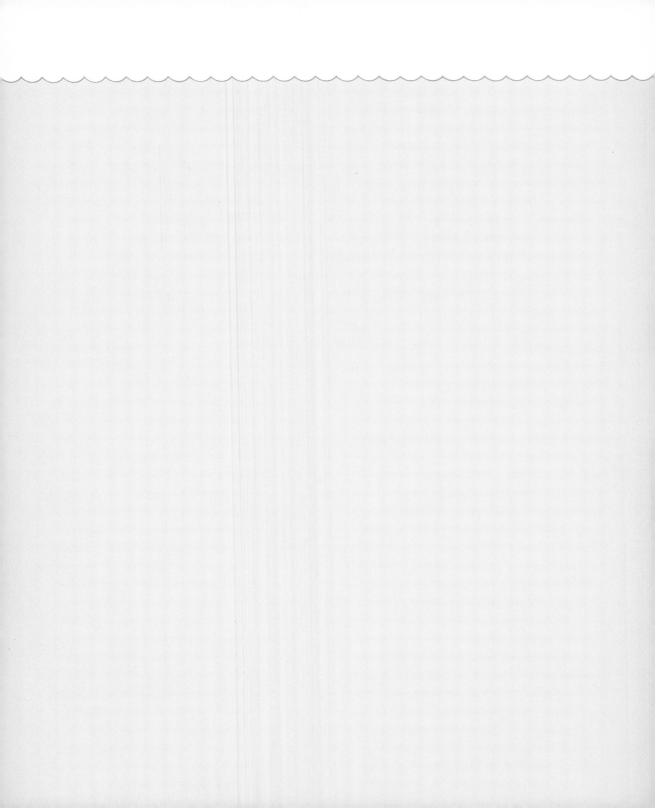

Appendix

Learning More about Diving and Underwater Archeology

1. Draw a mural on paper taped to a classroom wall. On the bottom, draw hills of sand. Scatter some treasure about, as well as some coins, gold chains, and wooden treasure chests brimming with emeralds, gold, and other jewels. Sketch sea creatures that live on the bottom—crabs, clams, oysters. Draw purple and yellow lacy fan corals that reach halfway to the top. Make mounds of coral. At the top, color the water lighter blue and draw in schools of striped fish swimming near the top. Add scuba divers, if you like, and a sunken ship.

2. If possible, visit Treasure Salvors Museum in Key West, Florida. Make a list of the treasure you see there. What do you consider the most interesting piece of treasure?

3. If you live near a maritime museum, ask a parent or guardian to take you there. See if you can identify different items in the museum. Can you tell what period of time they come from?

4. Visit a dive shop and ask the owner to explain some of the scuba diving equipment. Or, ask an adult or parent to help you use fins and snorkel. It's very easy, and lots of fun in the ocean, in a lake, in a pool, or even in the bathtub.

5. Draw a treasure map that shows where different pieces of the treasure of the *Atocha* were found. Be sure to include the mother lode, cannons, gold chains, emeralds, astrolabe, and other important items.

6. Make an atoll out of clay or other material. Put a shallow lagoon in the center. Place a beach around it, and then a reef. Add birds, trees, and bushes.

7. Go to a coin shop and ask if there are any Spanish coins from the seventeenth century. Walk through a city museum and look for seventeenth-century pottery, painting, jewelry, and clothing.

8. If you live near Delaware, visit the Delaware Technical and Community College in Georgetown. One of the investors in Mel Fisher's search for the *Atocha* donated all of his artifacts and much of his gold and jewels to the college. They are on display in a new museum at the college.

Glossary

airlift—a system of hoses used to remove sand covering objects underwater

ambergris (AM-buhr-gree)—a scented substance taken from the sperm whale; used by seventeenth-century travelers to fill pomanders—pleasant-smelling small bags or boxes

archeologist (ahr-kee-AHL-uh-gihst)—a scientist who studies artifacts to learn about past human life and activities

artifact—a tool, ornament, or other object from a particular time in the past

astrolabe (AS-troh-layb)—a navigational instrument used by a ship's pilot in the seventeenth century to calculate the position of the stars

atoll—a ring of islands surrounding a lagoon; most atolls are formed by volcanic islands that sink beneath the sea's surface, leaving a ring of coral reefs that, in time, become islands

ballast—the heavy objects, such as large stones, used to balance a ship in the water

bezoar (BEE-zohr) stone—a stone taken from the stomach of a goat or llama; ancient travelers believed the bezoar stone absorbed poison

bosun—on the *Atocha*, the ship's officer who was in charge of the hull and sails

bulwarks—the side of a ship above the upper deck

chain plate—a piece of rigging that supports the sails

drift pin—a small peg used to stretch the holes in the rigging of a sail

excavation (ehks-kuh-VAY-shuhn) site—used here to mean the place where archeologists dig

fossilized—preserved in petrified form; unchanged over a long period of time

grid—used here to mean a system of plastic pipes that looks like a tic-tac-toe board; it is set up over an excavation site

hull—the frame of a ship, without the sails or mast

ingot—metal melted into a block form for shipping

magnetometer (mag-nuh-TAH-muh-tuhr)—an instrument used to detect iron underwater; invented by Fay Feild

mailbox—an elbow-shaped steel tube which fits over a boat's propeller, forcing the water downward while the boat is anchored with engines running

manifest—the list of all cargo loaded onto a ship

marine archeologist—a scientist who studies shipwrecks and other remains in the sea to learn about past human life and activities

oxide—used here to describe the result of a chemical change which causes silver to turn black

photomosaic (foh-toh-moh-ZAY-ihk)—a complete photograph made from photographs of sections of a subject

rigging—lines and chains used aboard a ship to control sails and to support masts and spars

sediment—solid particles that settle to the bottom of a liquid

silt—loose sediment containing tiny rock particles or minerals

sonar—a device that uses sound waves to detect or measure the distance to other objects

stern—the rear of a boat

sterncastle—on the *Atocha*, the living quarters for rich passengers; the raised structure at the rear of a ship

theodolite (thee-AHD-uh-lyt) towers—towers fitted with telescope-like instruments for observing a boat's path across the water

Selected Bibliography

Books

Breeden, Robert L., ed. *Undersea Treasures*. Washington, D.C.: National Geographic Society, 1974.

Lyon, Eugene. *The Search for the* Atocha. Port Salerno, FL: Florida Classics Library, 1985.

Mathewson, R. Duncan, III. *Treasure of the* Atocha. New York: Pisces Books, 1986.

McClung, Robert M. *Treasures in the Sea*. Washington, D.C.: National Geographic Society, 1972.

Mohn, Peter B. *Scuba Diving and Snorkeling*. Mankato, MN: Crestwood House, 1980.

Sullivan, George. *The Modern Treasure Finder's Manual*. Radnor, PA: Chilton Press, 1975.

Articles

Dranov, Paula. "Hi-Tech Treasure Hunt." *Science Digest*, December 1982: 60+.

Lyon, Eugene. "*Atocha*, Tragic Treasure Galleon of the Florida Keys." *National Geographic*, June 1976: 787+.

Nordheimer, Jon. "Archeologists' Eyes Glittering Over Treasure." *New York Times*, July 24, 1985.

"Spanish Galleon's Timbers Made Accessible." *New York Times*, October 12, 1986.

Starr, Mark. "Treasure Hunt: Wrecks to Riches." *Newsweek*, August 5, 1985: 18-21.

Wilentz, Amy. "'We Found It! We Found It!' A Florida Team Discovers a Record Sunken Treasure, Lost in 1622." *Time*, August 5, 1985: 21-2.

Interviews

Fisher, Melvin. Telephone interview, March 2, 1987.

Mathewson, R. Duncan, III. Telephone interview, March 2, 1987.

Index